GRANDMOTHER
WHO . . .

GRANDMOTHER WHO . . .

Struggling with the Cruel Reality of Dementia

A Book of Poems by

GARI ANDREINI

With Contributions by Granddaughters
Megan and Hannah Hall

Edited by Dr. Sydney Newell

Library of Congress Control Number: 2020902707
ISBN: Hardcover   978-1-7960-8207-4
               Softcover   978-1-7960-8206-7
               eBook   978-1-7960-8205-0

With Contributions by Granddaughters Megan and Hannah Hall
Edited by Dr. Sydney Newell

Illustrated by: Windel Eborlas

Print information available on the last page.

Rev. date: 02/11/2020

To order additional copies of this book, contact:
Xlibris
1-888-795-4274
www.Xlibris.com
Orders@Xlibris.com
805770

PROLOGUE

Married to me for fifty-nine years, my wonderful and loving wife is suffering from advanced dementia.

She took care of me for nearly all of those years, raising two outstanding children and running the household while engaging in an exemplary career in the health-care field. I am now doing my best to take loving care of her for the time she has remaining.

I wrote the poems in this modest book to help deal with the pain of watching the glowing light slowly flicker out from the love of my life.

Each of our granddaughters contributed a poem as a tribute to her grandmother.

This poem was written by our granddaughter
Megan when she was starting high school.
I'm sharing her poem with you because it describes
her grandmother so lovingly and so well.

Grandparents and grandchildren have a sweet
alliance.

GRANDMOTHER WHO

Grandmother who bakes beautiful pecan pies and soft
angel food cake
and always takes the smallest piece;
who is sugar and sunshine;
who is a candle and a rose;
whose smile is bright,
is gentle in her every move;
who gave me dolls to play with;
who always has lemonade;
whose eyes are sweet and blue,
winks to say *I love you;*
got me bagels when I was young,
who got me coffee when I got older;
is quiet;
is always a gentle sea breeze;
is never mad;
nods her head in conversation;
is always putting me before her;
who will look in my eyes;
is patient with me;
who doesn't need words to say *I love you;*
is as sweet as the cakes she bakes—
everything she does says, *I love you.*
But have I told her, "I love you"?

Megan Hall

Upon hearing the news
that my loved one has dementia
with no hope of recovery

IT WILL BE A LONG GOODBYE

Wish you hadn't said that—
Therapist's duty assume

Six decades' worth
Fades away day by day by day

Wish you hadn't told me—
Messenger's burden it's said

Truth be damned
For love prevails

Oh were it so
As the lights grow dimmer still

Wish you hadn't said
But thankful for the know

Now we deal with the big picture:
Possibility,
Probability,
Eventuality,
$E=MC$ squared.
That may all be true,
But
What's for breakfast?

ETERNAL MENU

Ethereal soup after the *bang bang*
No atoms have ever been added
None to be deducted
Fourteen billion years to cook and expand
To be stirred and rearranged—
The same ingredients
But now with different names
So the question begs
Are we
But scrambled eggs?

Trying to clean out,

give away, or deal with

the many items my wife and I have in the house …

VASE

Picking it up from the shelf
Lonely and dusty

She bought it
Unable to use it now
No longer knows she has it

Downloading her treasures
Don't know how

It gets heavier
With misty eyes

Put it back on the shelf
To gather more dust

Not about graduation from high school

but rather from life itself.

A tribute to the Santa Rosa High School class of 1955

GRADUATION

What a time we've had
But soon, no more classes no more books

As graduation comes, the line advances
No more dates or Friday night lights

He's gone, she's gone,
And the line grows shorter

First it was Dutch, then Jack, then Sandy,
And it never stopped

One by one, two by two,
And the line grows shorter still

Who's next? We ask ourselves
"Certainly not I" we reason

As we wait our turn in the final procession
Before the next equation

Stage Two

ANGER

Robber, thief
Destroyer of life

You've taken away her memory
Leaving her to suffer

Stole her walking
I bot her a walker

Silenced her tongue
I kiss her and she smiles

Made her anxious
I gave her pills

Took her strength
I hired help

No longer can swallow food
So puree this, you fucker

Laugh if you will
But I'm here to stay

Some believe that bullfighting is an art and part of the Spanish culture
The drama of life and death played out in real life

But how does the bull feel about this?

VIDA

Tail against the curved wall
Safest place to be

Powerful now powerless
Blood drips to the ground

Fearless now fearful
Crowd cheers

Picadors retire
Banderillos too

Red illusion swirls
Make the charge

Flash of steel
Sudden pain

Momma he's hurting me
Now kneeling down

Lungs fill with blood
Peaceful darkness

Olé

Of the many nice things my wife said to me over the years,
one of the nicest might have been
about three years ago when she said to me, as things darkened for her,
"Thank you for sharing your life with me."

THE BALD MAN

The bald man is nice enough to me
Says he's my husband

But my husband is a much younger man
With black curly hair and bright blue eyes

What a time we had for over fifty years
Travele'd the world we did

From the Northern Lights
To the Southern Cross
And all those exciting places between

The bald man treats me tenderly
And cries when he doesn't see me looking

Soon my husband will come for me
I wait by the door for him to take me away

So I'll be saying goodbye to the bald man
Although he's nice enough to me

Aging comes with a price.

The question is are you willing to pay it?

Tollbooth or Early Exit?

Life's road we travel is full of wonder
Exciting scenery every mile

NO DEPOSIT NO RETURN

Exhilarated and challenged we speed along
With curves and bumps along the way

CAN'T GO BACK

Engine's missing a beat now and then
Grade becomes steeper still

WHAT LIES AHEAD

Tollbooth now in sight
Where silver and gold have no weight

MAY BE TOUGH TO TAKE

Fare to pay is godawful high
Why oh why does it have to be

THE CHOICE IS YOURS

Early exit on the right
Is only taken thoughtfully

BURMA-SHAVE

The psychological alliance between captors and their hostages can have many different forms

We are all captives in one way or another

SHADES OF STOCKHOLM SYNDROME

Patty-wacky

Please nurse

Student loan is due

Spousal beat

Back of the bus

You're in the army now

Into the truck girls

Ten to twenty

Thank you sir
May I please have another

Not accepting, but realizing

that I am powerless to stop this

LETTING GO

Traveling life's road together
Lifetime trip side by side

Exploring, experiencing, happy
Open road ahead

Together, always together, together

Car hits a bump—now she is outside
In rearview mirror

Image appears smaller and smaller
Can't stop—can't go back
Image fades away

Alone, alone

All alone

Farewell

to a setting sun.

(NOT) AFRAID

There is a ghost sliding on this hardwood floor
alongside my mother, but
I am not afraid.

I am accustomed to this walk of elegance —
my finger presses with ease on the mirror,
tracing their silhouettes —

minute and hour hands wired to meet
at every hour, and once when she winked,
we were convinced it wasn't an uncanny apparition.

It must have been the asparagus steam
that made her cry last month
and not her brain.

But you see, science fails to teach us what time offers:
how to love and preserve,
the changed.

It's difficult to admit there is a living life to mourn,
and maybe it would be easier to chase her spectral reflection
in every glass plane

to ignore the hardest part is yet to come.

My grandmother slides alongside us on these hardwood floors,
her shoes carving harmless ribbons of dust and goodbyes, and
I am afraid.

Hannah Hall

ACKNOWLEDGMENTS

I am grateful to the following people:

My therapist, Dr. Angela Huntsman, for encouraging me to write and express my emotions dealing with my wife's affliction with dementia.

My sister, Dr. Sydney Newell, for editing my little collection of poems.

Our two lovely granddaughters, Megan and Hannah Hall, for their poems (included in this collection) and for bringing so much happiness to our lives.

Milli, the love of my life.

Printed in the United States
By Bookmasters